I0576353

Caliburnus

by Annabelle Lewis

This book is a work of fiction. People, characters, places, events, and situations are the product of the author's imagination. Any resemblance to actual persons, living or dead, or historical events, is purely coincidental.

Contact Annabelle at: annabellelewisauthor@gmail.com
Website: https://www.theannabellelewis.com
https://www.facebook.com/AnnabelleLewisAuthor
https://twitter.com/alewisauthor

ISBN-13: 978-0-9993368-9-2 (Ebook)
ISBN-13: 978-1-7343757-01 (Paperback)

First Edition

Publisher: PePe Press
Editing and Interior Designer: Pikko's House

Novels by Annabelle Lewis

The Carrows Family Chronicles

Charlotte McGee

Titan Takedown

Carrows Justice

The Bad Penny

Fisher of Men

DEDICATION

For special needs parents everywhere. We dream.

Chapter One

One summer day, Vivian Rees sat on the dock of her lake home and stared at her son, Pinocchio, currently buried in the sand. She squinted, focusing on his face, and saw a mysterious look of contentment. His head, as usual, was topped with a small red-felt hat.

A breeze from nowhere made Vivian start, concerned for the safety of the hat. What if it blew away? How far would it travel?

She looked at the sky, trying to determine if bad weather was coming their way. But the day was perfectly calm, a blue-sky day in paradise, typically quiet for mid-week, vacant of the workaday crowd that busied the waters on the weekends.

Vivian dangled her feet in the water and brushed back a tear. *Stop it,* she scolded herself. *It is what it is. You can't change it. You can't do anything other than help*

him stay calm and find happiness. And take him to doctors.
Shit loads of doctors.

Just last month, the neurologist, kind and well-intentioned, though wildly off the mark in her delivery, had said, "We might be looking at a brain tumor." That had knocked Vivian back. If her world had been challenging before, with all the autism specialists clamoring about their day, it came to a screeching halt in that moment.

She looked over at her four-year-old son. His real name, of course, was not Pinocchio. It was Jesse. The most beautiful, angelic-looking blond-headed kid ever born. Interesting too, when he finally did begin to utter his first few words at three, that his voice was a unique tone of raspy. Vivian adored it, but then, the more she thought about it, she supposed it could be attributed to all the screaming poor Jesse did to get through each sensory-overloaded horror of a day.

Everything in his world was just too much. His brain was overloaded, unable to filter out noise or process light. Or the feel of wet grass beneath his bare feet, the feel of a soft touch—the list was endless. The sand, however, the weight of it, the tightness encasing his small body, made him feel good. And that was a gift.

Vivian had buried him in the sand over two hours ago. And still he sat, staring, content, thinking about... what? She'd applied generous amounts of sunblock, the wailing, screaming battle to apply it typical and exhausting but necessary. He'd brought the shovel to her, and she'd dug the hole. After burying him sitting crisscross applesauce in the sand, she dragged a beach umbrella out of their boathouse and stuck it next to her boy and his mound to shade him.

But for how many more hours? If he was happy, she should let him be, but nature was calling, and there was no way she could leave him buried in the sand on a deserted Minnesota beach and run up to the house to use the bathroom. She shook her head and looked at the water, the obvious solution.

"I'm going in the water, Pie," she yelled over to her son, not expecting a response. She got none as she waded into the cool, almost cold, but refreshing water and walked slowly out.

After all the horrific tests they'd gone through, and all the steps they'd taken to garner participation from her wild, unruly, unreachable patient, she told herself she should just be grateful that there was no stinking tumor. But then again, she'd had moments going through the what-ifs. She'd lain awake at night wondering if it was a tumor. And if it was successfully removed, would it cure him? Open up some blockage, some neurological pathways, some jammed-up, gummed-up system, and he would be free?

But it wasn't a tumor. It was just god-awful autism. Oh, and maybe absence seizures. Whatever. Those tests could wait until they got back from their time together at the beach.

Vivian felt the smooth, velvety sand between her toes and marveled, looking down at how crystal clear the water was. They were lucky to own such a place, on such a beautiful beach. They were lucky about a lot of things. "Blessed" was her focus word for the month. She had charms with the damn word written on it all over the house, even carried one in her purse, and in her pocket. But it was hard.

She shouted again, "Jeeesseee. The water feels soooo good. Do you want to take a break and swim with me?"

"Nocchio."

She recognized the sharp verbal output. It was a correction. His mangled reminder that his name was not Jesse.

He'd never accepted his identity. As a human. As a boy. He'd always been a character. He'd worn costumes since he had the ability to dictate his preferences. Not too untypical for a kid, but the month he'd been an elephant—the dangling towel taped to his nose, a second towel in his pants for a tail—had been challenging. The towels had gotten in the way. Bathing was a nightmare, for the obvious reasons. It was hard to bathe with towels.

Then there was Gumby. Jesse's fingers splayed directly in half, forming the perfect imitation. It was hard to eat or do things with your hands when you were Gumby. T-Rex had been easier—at least with his pointer and middle finger in claws, he could use them to eat.

Vivian pulled off her hat and, holding it in the air so it would not get wet, she submersed herself completely, letting the water cleanse her as she went under. *Brrr, it's cold,* she thought as she popped back to the surface, her first look to the nearby shore to check on Jesse. Pinocchio.

This character had lasted the longest. He'd been Pinocchio for almost a year now, and she lived in constant fear of losing Pinocchio's red-felt hat. That fear had begun after it flew out the car window when she'd accidently hit the wrong window control. Jesse, in the backseat, had been hysterical. Her husband was out of town, and it was nighttime. She'd rushed back home to find a flashlight, Jesse screaming bloody murder, pounding his head against the car seat and the window. The two of them drove back to the dark stretch of road where the event had happened. She put on the hazard lights and got out and searched. She'd found it, but she'd been frightened of losing it ever since. It owned them all.

She should feel grateful, *blessed*, that at least Pinocchio could use his hands. Jesse had found the odd red-felt hat and matching vest on some large doll, and when donned, he declared himself morphed, like magic, into Pinocchio. The boy was gone…again, this time, ironically, into a wooden boy longing to become real.

The cruelness of that irony made her heart break. Tucking him in at night, propping his hat on his head just so, her "Nocchio" would hold her arm under the weight of the blankets while she read him the story of the wooden boy. Night after night after night.

Unable to care for himself, Jesse was still in diapers, and Vivian was the only person in the world who understood his daily needs to cope. What, dear

God, was going to happen to him?

Vivian looked around and began to hammer the water. She yelled again at the beach, trying to elicit a response, "I'm splashing, I'm splashing." She yelled louder, "Look, Jesse, I'm splashing!"

Again, a small cry. The short guttural correction. *Blessed, dammit!*

Vivian let the water quiet around her waist and considered its depths. Standing still, she peered at a shiny object. *Hmm, what is that?*

She reached down with her hand but realized that she couldn't get to it without going under. She pulled her white floppy hat off her head again and held it in the air as her face entered the water, her eyes wide open as she easily saw again the brilliant object. In the total silence of the underwater world, her senses changed. For a moment, she was somewhere else as her hand slowly moved toward the object. She touched it and released it from the sand.

She rose up from the water and looked at it in the air. It was a ring. A silverish ring. Maybe it was completely silver, but it seemed old. Like steel but not terribly tarnished. It had a bright cast to it, and the sun glinted off of it brightly. Vivian rolled it between her fingers and examined it as she waded through the water toward the sandy beach. She plowed her feet forward, all drippy and wet, and went over to Jesse under the umbrella.

"Look. Look what I found in the water. It's a ring. A silver ring. Do you see it?" she said, forcing it into his line of sight. He looked. His arms free, resting atop the pile of sand, he put out a tentative finger and quickly touched it.

"It's sparkly, isn't it? Do you want to wear it?" she said, demonstrating with her own finger and admiring it. She pulled it off and picked up his hand.

"Noooooo," he said in his raspy voice.

"Okay," she said, immediately hurt that once again she couldn't engage with him. "I'll wear it myself." She put it on her left hand's ring finger and lay next to him. Her hair and body were going to be full of sand. She'd need to go back in the water, but that was okay. She sighed as she realized it was time to negotiate the transition. It might take hours to get him out of the sand, but she had to start somewhere.

She talked to him, and he let her. For now, it was what they had, and it was enough.

Vivian's husband and Jesse's father, Grant, was in the city, which made the trip to the lake house alone with Jesse very hard. She had to do everything by herself, and it could be a very physical job. She was nervous quite a lot that one false move would set off a tantrum. One green bowl not in position, the food not prepared and presented exactly the same as it was supposed to be, could unleash a terrible ordeal. Vivian was always careful in her planning, and from the moment she woke every morning, the list-making and the complicated game of chess began. All to keep him calm.

Lots of people, most of them well-meaning, had

opinions about the way Vivian and Grant managed Jesse. Most of them were stupid. They had no idea what it was like to live with a child with autism. Vivian and Grant had been taught to think of their life with their son through the lens of a traffic signal. You had to pick your battles. Red-light goals such as brushing your teeth, or wearing your seatbelt, or banging your head against the wall and floor were worked on. They were told to keep the list of red-light issues to a minimum. Yellow-light goals such as eating healthier foods, making him use his words instead of gesturing, were yellow—sometimes you went for it, sometimes you didn't. All the rest went straight through the green light.

Well-meaning folk thought there should be many, many more than three red-light issues at a time. If there weren't more, then the Reeses were giving in to Jesse's demands; they were coddling him, reinforcing the behavior and rewarding him. Those people were definitely stupid.

That night, finally up from the beach and in pajamas, Jesse was watching a horrible children's video for the ten thousandth time while Vivian made herself a sandwich. Opening a bottle of wine, however, was her first priority. She pulled out the opener and got to work on removing the foil wrapper with a knife. One aggressive move later, the knife slipped and jammed into her hand.

"Dammit," she said. She threw the knife on the counter and inspected the wound. It was painful but not too bad. She walked to the faucet and ran cold water on it. Blood poured out, not an alarming amount, but enough that she knew she would need a Band-Aid. She went into the bathroom and doctored it up, having to use several bandages to keep it in place.

Unconcerned, she got back to her work, opened the bottle, and poured a glass. Ah, elixir. She'd have to do the dishes to make sure his special breakfast bowl was clean after she ate. She looked at her hand and frowned. That could be a messy problem. No way around it, though. There was no dishwasher, and the dishes had to be done.

They were leaving the following morning. Jesse had an appointment in the city with his occupational therapist, and that would not be missed. She looked at him, his Barney jammas on, his blond hair still damp from his bath, the red-felt vest and hat in place. He was singing along with the song. She could tell that, but his words were not formed; they were tonal inflections. But he had the song memorized and right.

Blessed.

That night, she put him to bed, performing the bedtime ritual perfectly, getting under the mound of covers with him to read the book. The pressure of the piles of blankets gave him comfort and made him sleepy. Both of them, really.

Vivian yawned as she read the children's version of the condensed book, "And the Blue Fairy said, in order to be a real boy, you must beeeee……"

"Ave, uthfu, asefish," Jesse said, working his throat muscles to form the words *brave, truthful, unselfish*.

"That is perfect," Vivian said, giving him a kiss on the head.

Finishing the book and turning off the lamp, Vivian decided to call it a night herself. No reason to leave the comfortable cocoon either. She grabbed Jesse's hand under the covers and held it.

They fell asleep just like that.

Chapter Two

The next morning, they made their way into the city and directly to the OT appointment. Vivian read a parenting magazine as Jesse and Kelsey, the therapist, came back into reception. Disheartened and troubled by the article on how toilet training for boys should be accomplished by eighteen months, she threw it down and stood to meet them.

"Great session," said Kelsey as Jesse ran to her and hugged her around the knees. Vivian smiled and placed a protective hand on his hat and head.

"Great!"

"No," Kelsey said, her brows furrowed, "I mean really great. He was compliant, but more than that, he just went through the exercises perfectly. Like he finally got it. The actions where he needs to cross mid-line? He just did it. Like it was no effort at all." Kelsey referred to crossing the imaginary mid-line drawn from the head to the feet, which separates the body. Working across a mass of tissue called the corpus callosum, both the left and right hemispheres of the brain needed to work together in order to accomplish it.

Vivian smiled, pleased that something was going in the right direction. "That's wonderful."

Kelsey shook her head. "And then when we were on the trampoline, he had no trouble at all standing on one leg and balancing. I even jumped a little, and he held it," she said as she looked down. Jesse was staring at Kelsey.

"He's looking at you," Vivian whispered as she felt a lump in her throat.

"He's *staring* at me," Kelsey said with awe. "Straight in the eyes."

Vivian got on her knees and looked at her son. He didn't back away. He didn't run away or scream in pain to be released, he just looked into her eyes and smiled.

He was there.

"Hi there, Jesse," Vivian said softly, her eyes filling with tears.

"I," he rasped, still looking at her.

She grabbed his face in both hands, held his forehead next to hers, and stared defiantly into them, completely invading his space. She felt him struggle slightly, but then he kissed her quickly and put his hands over hers, pulling them down.

She released him and sat back on her heels as Jesse ran over to a play table and began stacking blocks. She started crying, her face in her hands, and rocked as Kelsey knelt beside her and put an arm around her shoulders. "He's doing really well, Mrs. Rees. It's been a good day."

Vivian nodded and collected herself. She and Jesse went home.

Back in the routine of their Minneapolis home, Jesse was content, surrounded by his toys, everything familiar. His LEGOs were laid out in a recognizable pattern, comforting and meaningful only to Jesse. With various objects, he'd recreated the shape of something resembling a figure wherever he went. The figures lay on floors in rooms throughout the house and were never to be disturbed.

Vivian sat at the kitchen table next to Grant. He'd brought home a pizza. They were both drinking wine.

"That's great," said Grant, swallowing some pizza after Vivian told him about therapy.

She glanced briefly at Jesse and watched him in the next room, swaying to a song, singing the familiar lyrics to his favorite music. She stared at her hand and rubbed her thumb over the spot that only the night before had been injured. There was nothing there.

"It is great," she said absently, frowning, trying to remember how bad the cut had been in the first place. Shouldn't there be something there?

"What's wrong?" he said.

"I cut my hand last night, and it's gone. It's healed."

"Uh-huh," he said, dishing up more salad. "How'd you cut it?"

"Frantically opening a bottle of wine." She smiled at him.

"Huh." He grinned. "Like the time you sliced your hand opening the yoga CD. I guess you had it coming," he teased.

"Yeah. I guess I did." She stared again at Jesse. His foot knocked a couple small LEGOs out of place in his creation on the floor. He looked back at her and smiled.

Chapter Three

Things, small things, didn't add up. Grant let her sleep in the next morning and volunteered to get up when they heard Jesse making noises. But that wasn't the weird part. That came when Vivian went downstairs and found Jesse and Grant on the floor, rolling a ball between them, playing a floor game of catch.

"Yay!" Grant said, scooting backward to increase the distance.

"Yay!" Jesse said, as he fist-pumped and mimicked his dad.

The game continued as Vivian stood there, beaming.

But then she saw the bowl. It wasn't green, it was blue. Jesse would only eat from green bowls. That had been going on forever. And not just any green bowl, but a particular kind and shape. Vivian had purchased it at a Tupperware party. It came in a set with three other identical plastic bowls of pink, yellow, and blue. Once Jesse had latched on to the green Tupperware bowl as one of his lifelines, she'd ordered three more sets, so she'd have spare green ones to use.

"Did he eat out of a blue bowl?" she asked Grant, uncertain if she was happy or annoyed that Grant had gotten it wrong or incredulous that he'd gotten away with it.

"Yeah," Grant said, coming into the kitchen. "I just pulled one down, and he didn't fuss. I didn't even notice until after he'd finished."

"What the heck?" Vivian squished up her face. "That's unbelievable."

"Get this," said Grant, pouring himself a cup of coffee. "He also tried a blueberry."

"What?" Her jaw dropped.

"Yeah," he said, holding his cup. "I put one of mine in front of him and told him to try it. And he did."

"Then what happened?" she said, her jaw still open.

Grant smiled and took a sip. He shrugged. "Nothing. He just ate it."

"Wow." She walked to the kitchen table and sat, still in her robe. She pointed to the coffee and Grant grabbed a cup. He brought it to the table and took a seat.

She pulled it toward her and picked it up just as Jesse came rushing into the room and grabbed her. The cup upended, pouring scalding coffee onto her hand as both she and Grant lunged to grab it in slow motion.

"Ow!" she exclaimed as Grant plucked Jesse out of the way. Vivian stood up and grabbed a wad of paper napkins sitting nearby and threw it down on the coffee. She made her way to the sink to run the burn under cold water.

Grant, wiping the table, said, "Is it bad?"

"Come here," she said.

Grant got there fast.

"Look," she said quietly. She'd pulled her hand out of the water. An angry burn the size of a lemon was on the back of her hand. "It hurt really bad, and then it just stopped. It feels fine," she said, flexing it.

They peered at the hand, and together, they watched the angry red patch return to normal coloring as if nothing had happened.

She kept flexing it, staring at her left hand, considering it.

"What the heck? I guess you're a fast healer," he said as he gave her a supportive pat on the back.

"No, Grant, it's totally strange. You didn't see it at first. There should be something there. It's only been a minute. There was a burn. And it hurt, and then it didn't."

"You're *blessed*, babe," he said as he walked over to the table and resumed cleaning.

"Grant, stop," she said as she walked over to him. "I'm not kidding. This is weird. That's twice I've healed super quick. It's got to mean something."

"I'm sure it does, but I wouldn't get worked up

over it. You've got good genes," he said as he threw the rest of the wet napkins in the trash. "It should come in handy if you ever really get hurt."

"I'm not waiting," she said as she marched over to a cabinet near the dining room and pulled out her sewing kit. She brought it back to the table and sat down.

"What are you doing?" Grant said, watching her pull out a needle.

She looked him. "Sit down, we need to witness this together. I'm going to stab myself and see what happens."

"The *hell*, honey," he said with a concerned look. "Are you kidding?"

"No. Now sit."

He sat.

"Here we go." She took the needle and sharply poked her finger.

"You didn't sterilize it," he said with alarm as they watched the finger immediately bleed.

Vivian grabbed another napkin and patted the small amount of blood away. Nothing replaced it. She squeezed it. No blood came. She looked at Grant, a little dizzy.

"Wow," he said. "That was impressive."

"Let me do you." She grabbed his hand and stabbed him before he had a chance to react.

"Ow!" he said as he pulled back his hand and shot her a look of annoyance. But he put his hand back between them and looked at the blood pooling on his finger. He grabbed the napkin and wiped it away.

More blood replaced it. He wiped again, and less came this time. He squeezed it. It bled a lot.

"That's what's supposed to happen," she said.

"Maybe you didn't stab yours as hard as you did mine," he said, still annoyed.

"The hell, Grant?" Vivian glared at him. She held the needle high and then forcefully stabbed her finger again, hard. She received the same result. It hurt, but there was minimal blood flow, and it went away almost immediately.

"Well, this was fun," he said, irritated as he went to the bathroom. "Where are the bandages?" he yelled.

She followed him there and dove under the cabinet for the box. "Grant, I think something big is happening here. You don't understand."

He doctored his hand at the sink as she turned and closed the lid on the toilet and sat. She put her left hand out and stared at the ring. "I found this ring in the lake yesterday. It's steel, or silver, I'm not sure. Grant. What if the ring is doing this?"

Grant wrapped his finger in the bandage and looked at her. "What are you talking about?"

Her heartbeat ticked up. "This ring," she said, holding it up for him to look at. "I found it in the lake. I put it on, and since then, weird things have been happening. Jesse is better," she said in a shaky voice. Tears pooled in her eyes.

Grant put his hands on her shoulders. "Don't do this, Vivian. Stop. There's no magic ring. He's just had a good day."

She shook her head violently, her face contorted. Her body began to tremble.

"Come here," he said, hoisting her up and holding her. "It's okay," he said as she began to cry.

"But what if it's true?" she said, sobbing into his chest. "What if I found a magic ring?"

"Then I guess you won the lotto. Come on. Stop crying. It's okay."

She pushed him back. "I've got to know," she said. "How can I know?"

"Know if you have a magic ring?"

She grabbed a tissue and blew her nose, "Yes. Exactly. We have to test it."

"What kind of test?" he said, giving his head a small shake.

"I don't know! Let's think of something." She pushed past him, her adrenaline rushing, and went into the living room, where Jesse was still dancing to his music. She grabbed the remote and put the video on pause—an unbelievable, unforgivable sin in her son's eyes. She waited for him to react.

He did. He pointed. With a single index finger stretched out at the remote, he said, "Go."

She hit play. He resumed his dance. Vivian stared at Grant, defiant, and walked toward him. "That should have sent him into outer space. You know that. And he used his pointing finger," she said, covering her mouth. "He's never done that."

Grant ran his hand over the side of his face, confused. Vivian, her robe flying behind her, ran back into the kitchen and started opening drawers.

"What are you doing?" Grant said, following her, alarmed.

"Where are the matches? The lighter. I'm going to burn my hand again."

"Stop," he said, going to her, grabbing her by the shoulders. "You're not going to burn yourself. Stop this."

She stared at him. "You're right. Let's burn you first," she said as she resumed her hunt.

"Vivian, slow down. Stop. No burning. Stop this!" he said as he looked out on Jesse.

"Okay," she said as she slammed another drawer shut. "How about a hammer? I'll break my toe. Let's see what happens then." She ran to the garage.

"This is bullshit," he said as he followed her.

She grabbed the hammer off the peg.

"You're not doing this," he said.

"Watch me," she said as she sat on the garage floor, hammer in hand.

BAM! She brought it down hard on her big toe.

Two things happened at once. She screamed and threw the hammer aside. She grabbed her toe as Grant ran to her, screaming her name.

"What have you done?" he yelled.

Vivian's eyes went wide. She released her toe, and they looked at it together. "It stopped," she whispered. "The pain. It was immediate, but it stopped. And look," she said, wiggling her toe. "It's perfect."

To say the rest of the day was normal would be

wrong, but Vivian did not purposefully injure herself again. What they did was test Jesse. Test after test after test. They used his self-imposed triggers against him, and almost every time, he coped. There were no tantrums. None. There was flexibility. There was joy, and interaction, and blessed, beautiful eye contact. And there were words. Not many, but they came. He tried, and they came.

Vivian paced the kitchen as she and Grant thought about the day.

"I slept with him the night before last. All night. And I held his hand with my hand, the one wearing the ring."

"And you think you healed him," he said, rubbing his forehead.

"My God. I can't imagine. I can't believe it. But what if it's true? What if it has healing power?" She walked over to the table and splayed her hand on it. They stared at the ring.

"Get a magnifying glass," she said.

Grant went to his study and came back with one. She removed the ring, and they each took a turn examining it. "It looks like writing there," he said. "Or like an etching or a pattern, but it's worn down. I can't make it out."

"I can't either. You put it on," she said.

Grant looked at her and obliged, but it only went as far as the first knuckle on his pinkie finger. "You're not going to hit me with a hammer now, are you?" he said, raising an eyebrow.

"Should I?"

He rolled his eyes. "No."

"We have to test it. Come on. Don't be a baby," she said as she got the sewing kit out again.

He presented his hand, palm up. She took hold of it and came down hard with the needle into the pad of his middle finger. It bled.

"Ow!" he said, jerking it back.

They repeated the performance from the morning, but Grant's finger responded the same as it had before. It bled a lot and continued to when they squeezed it. He took off the ring off his knuckle and gave it to her as he held a napkin on it for pressure. "Guess it doesn't work for me."

She slid it back on her hand. "Maybe it's because you couldn't get it on all the way. Or maybe because you weren't the one who found it."

"Whatever," he said. "I can't believe we're even discussing this."

She folded her arms across her chest. "I get it. I do. But I'm keeping an open mind on this, Grant."

"On magic. On your magic healing ring."

"Yes."

They stared at one another, long-time friends and partners, and compassionately read their cues. He nodded and sighed. "Okay, I will too."

That night they lay in bed, and she held his hand in her left. "You got a headache or anything there we can test, sweetheart?" she teased.

"Can't say that I do," he said, rolling over, his hands reaching out to her.

"Grant," she said, putting a hand on his chest, "if

23

it's magic. And it cures. If we know it can cure, then what am I supposed to do with that?"

"You mean, like a responsibility?"

"Yes. If I can cure people, I mean if the ring can cure people, then what are we supposed to do?"

Grant rolled back over. "I don't know," he said into the dark. "Honestly. I don't."

They lay quiet, considering. Her voice softly said, "Would it be selfish if I kept it for Jesse? In case, like, he needs it some more. Like another dose or something? Or what if something happens to him, or you, or me, and we need it? What if it only has so much power, like only a few doses? Maybe I've wasted some of its magic on my finger and my stupid toe?"

"How can we know? We can't. We could have the ring studied. Like figure out what it's made of. I know someone at work whose wife is a chemist. Maybe she could take a look at it."

"Like put it through chemical tests? What if it's made of something from outer space? Something they haven't seen before? Then what? They won't give it back, that's for sure."

"Jesus. A magic ring, on the shores of Pelican Lake."

"Speaking of Jesus, this could be a gift from God," she said quietly.

"I suppose it could be."

"We have a responsibility, then, Grant. I don't think we can keep it for ourselves."

"You mean give it away?"

"No, I mean we need to use it."

Grant flipped on the light and sat up. "Use it. You mean to heal people?"

Vivian nodded into her pillow and looked at him. "Yes."

He looked away. "I guess that could be a test."

"Who do we know that's sick?"

Chapter Four

The next day, Sunday, before the three of them headed out to Grant's sister's house, Jesse was once again cooperative, flexible, and miraculously responsive. Grant and Vivian worked hard to hold back the tears of joy as they went through their morning routine.

"Muffin was diagnosed with cancer last week," Grant said as they made their exit off the freeway. "Not a person, but you could hold her for a long time. Cecelia said she's moving but seems really tired," he said, referring to his sister's beagle.

"She's what, four? Ceci's not going to do anything medical soon, or put Muffin down, is she?"

"She said she couldn't afford the surgery, and she was just going to keep her comfortable until it was time."

Vivian looked out the window, scared to death.

Did the ring contain the power to heal cancer? How long did she need to hold the dog for it to work? She had no idea.

"All right, Muffin. Hang on, here we come."

They had a nice visit with Ceci and her family, and of course, Vivian spent an inordinate amount of time holding Muffin. Her left hand with the ring rubbed the spot where the tumor laid on her chest. They went home to wait.

Monday, Grant called Vivian with the news that the lab lady, his co-worker's wife, and he had exchanged e-mails. She said she'd be happy to look at the ring whenever they wanted. She gave her address at the lab and her hours of business. She told them to pop by and she'd be around.

"I had a thought," Grant said into the phone. "What if it's not the ring at all, and it's just you?"

"You mean that I'm a fast healer? Are we going there again?"

"No, that the ring isn't the thing, but it's, like, you. That you've got a gift."

Vivian sat on the sofa, Jesse next to her. He was reading *The Cat in the Hat* to her. His inflection and rhythm were spot on, and this time, a few more of the words were fully formed. And he was calm. But the biggest thing was that he'd left his red-felt hat off his head, where it had fallen, across the room. She stared at the hat and felt herself tremble. She didn't know what to believe.

"I can take it off, but how do we test that hypothesis? Should I get the hammer?"

"Christ, no," his voice rose. "We'll talk about this when I get home. Listen to me. No more hammers."

"No hammers. Got it."

Vivian and Grant sat at the dinner table with Jesse. Unprecedented for any length of time, he squirmed around in his chair but smiled at them and stayed as he tried to use his utensils—a feat his fine-motor skills had been unable to accomplish. He speared a pear successfully and looked at it with a satisfied expression. He popped it into his mouth and chewed.

"I can't wait," Vivian said as she reached for her phone. "I'm calling Ceci."

"Hey, girl," said Vivian as Grant got up and retrieved some dessert.

"Wondering how Muffin has been today. Poor little girl." Vivian listened as she watched Grant open the brownies and cut a small piece. He handed it to Jesse, who was pointing at them calmly and saying, "pease."

Her eyes got wide. "Huh. That's wonderful."

Vivian mouthed *oh my god* and eventually disconnected.

"Muffin's better," she said.

"What's she doing different?"

"She ate and played like a pup all day. Ceci was thrilled. I mean, obviously."

"Huh," Grant said, biting the corner of a nail. "We'll have to check again tomorrow."

"Yeah," she said as she cleared the table.

"Now what?" he said, following her with dishes.

"Now we find a person. Someone really sick. Like in a hospital. A child, maybe. Do we know anyone?"

"I don't. But Scottish Rite Children's is down the street."

"So, I go troll the hallways and hold some strange kid's hand? For how long? Why would they let me? I can't get to the patients."

They racked their brains. What to do. What to do.

Chapter Five

Tuesday morning came, and while Vivian felt completely distracted, she forced herself to participate in their normal routine. She brought Jesse to the occupational therapist, Kelsey, for their scheduled appointment. She watched Jesse go back to the therapy rooms, willingly and happily. She was overwhelmed with the love she felt for him. She sat down and closed her eyes in the empty reception, trying again not to cry in public, when the door flew open. A woman, a terrible woman who Vivian couldn't stand, walked in with her eight-year-old son.

Constance *"call-me-Connie"* Spengali gave Vivian a simpering smile and said, "How's your Jesse today?"

"He's good," said Vivian, this being the traditional question Connie asked each time they ran into each other at therapy.

"I'll just pop back and drop off Tony," she said

as she walked through the door and back toward the therapy rooms unescorted.

Vivian rolled her eyes, dreading the thought of having to spend the next hour alone with Connie while they waited for their children to receive therapy. Not Connie. Not today. She groaned.

But Connie Spengali returned and took a seat next to Vivian, grabbing her hand—her left hand—and giving it a big squeeze. She launched in. "You're not going to believe how much progress Tony is making in school. Let me tell you."

Connie shook her head dramatically as she put her purse on the floor and pulled out a piece of paper. "I'm so happy I ran into you today. Listen," she said as she passed the paper over to Vivian, "I made a list for you of those books I told you about potty training. I really think if you applied yourself and used the tools in these books, you'd have him trained. He'll be in kindergarten next year, right? He cannot go to school in diapers, Vivian."

Vivian fumed as Connie grabbed her left hand again and held it. "Vivian, I'm here to help you. I hope you're not taking this as a criticism. My Tony, he's just doing so well, I want to share our success with everyone. Really. I'm available if you want to discuss this stuff. Just give me a call. Have you and your husband discussed having a therapy room installed in your home yet? My Tony just thrived; major advancements were made after we started working the program with him at home. Believe me, I was not keen to put a bolster swing in the middle of our living room, but it's worked miracles. Of course, that was before the money." She waved her hand through the air. "I think—" Connie looked around at the empty room and squeezed Vivian's hand harder. "—Tony is very close to a cure. I'm completely encouraged."

Vivian had been listening to Connie's lectures about how she was fixing her son's autism for the last year. Her face reddened as her mind flipped through the memories, recalling all the hurtful bullshit Connie had said to her. During that time, Jesse hadn't been getting better at all. The gap had been widening. Tony was getting better. Some kids made progress, and some didn't. The degrees to which the horrible affliction would affect them came in a range. Jesse had been toward the bottom, and Tony was, according to Connie, with the help of her strategies, working his way toward the high-functioning end of the spectrum.

But today was different. Vivian had a reason, an effing magical reason, to hope. "I'll look them over," Vivian said, releasing her hand.

"Call me if you want to talk." Connie laughed. "Did I tell you about my Emily? My goodness! She's been placed in the key program! For the gifted and talented! She's a complete genius." Connie winked. "Just like her father."

Steve, Connie's husband, was an aerospace engineer. Vivian had heard all about his patent and the money that was rolling into the Spengalis' coffers as a result. They'd moved into a gated community— into the largest home—and a play therapist worked with Tony full time. That... and the indoor pool... and the private occupational therapy room… Connie had all the answers to curing autism.

The vexing conversation continued as the hour went by, and Tony was the first one brought out. He ran past his mother and straight over to the tank and began to count the fish—a ritual they'd all witnessed after every session.

Connie smiled indulgently at Vivian and held out her arms. Vivian smiled and walked into them as Connie said, "Hang in there, Vivian. Just try to remember that Jesse is worth it."

Vivian felt her face redden, and hate flooded through her at the implication that she may have somehow decided that Jesse wasn't worth it.

Mercifully, Connie left as Jesse and Kelsey came into reception. It was another repeat performance, as Kelsey emoted about Jesse's accomplishments. The two of them reveled in the progress. Genuine happiness flooded once again into Vivian's heart as she left therapy with her son. She was fully convinced that they'd been given a miracle.

At home that night, she and Grant shared the details of their day, still undecided about what to do next. Vivian texted Ceci, who happily reported that Muffin had had another terrific day.

They tossed around the options and decided to do something crazy. They would stake out the hospital and see if they could get to a patient at the children's hospital. They booked a babysitter for the following day. Grant would take the afternoon off.

Chapter Six

The two of them entered the lobby of Scottish Rite. Having been there a number of times with Jesse, Vivian and Grant were familiar with the layout. What was always startling was the sheer number of desperate, heart-breaking children who filled the waiting room. Blind children, deformed, in wheelchairs, sick. It felt like puppies were being murdered all around them.

"Let's sit in the waiting room for a bit and see what happens," Vivian said as they took two chairs.

Grant grabbed a magazine off a nearby table. "I'll try to look innocuous," he said under his breath.

Vivian glanced at the cover of the inappropriate parenting magazine left in a room of parents who were parenting their hearts out. The model-perfect mother and toddler on the cover rode over the caption— "76 Tips for Being a Chill Mom."

Vivian shook her head. It was so insulting. A young couple nearby looked haggard. In their early twenties, they had what must be twins, as both children appeared to be the same age, about two. Both children, two girls, wore helmets. Vivian watched the family periodically while pretending to be engaged in her phone.

Check out those two, she texted Grant.

He pulled out his phone and texted back. *Twins?*

She nodded.

The twins' dad, wearing worn jeans and a Lynyrd Skynyrd T-shirt, looked wiped-out tired. His eyes were closed, and his head did the fast jerk of someone who had quickly recovered from falling asleep.

Vivian got up and wandered over to them, looking at a selection of magazines on a nearby rack. Ugh. The options pissed her off. She heard the woman whisper to her husband. "How are you going to make it through the day?"

The Skynyrd guy said, "If I could get a couple hours, I'd be okay. Isn't there somewhere I could lay down while we wait?"

Vivian grabbed a magazine whose cover read, "30 Great Ideas on How to be an In-the-Moment Mom!" She sat in an empty chair next to the haggard mom, who also wore jeans and a T-shirt, hers sporting a wet spot near the collar.

Vivian feigned reading the article but then leaned over and pointed to the cover. "In-the-Moment Mom. Gotta love it, right?"

Haggard Mom glanced at the cover and shook her

head. "I don't even know what that means."

Vivian flipped through the pages and looked at the two girls who sat in front of them. One was asleep in a stroller, her head in her helmet lolling to the side. The other sat on the floor. She'd turned over her stroller and was busy spinning the wheels, her hand slapping at them, making them go round. Both girls' dark hair was cut short, small curls barely visible at the bottom of the helmets, which was probably why the mom dressed them both in pink. The T-shirt on the twin playing with the wheels said, "I'm Two Cute" — an apparent nod to the fact that she was two. The asleep twin's pink T-shirt said one word "Blessed."

Vivian froze as she stared at the shirt and sleeping toddler, the child's face angelic in repose. "Your children are beautiful," she said to the mom.

"Thank you."

"Are you waiting for neurology?" Vivian asked, taking a leap and assuming their appointment was to address a problem with epilepsy.

"Yes. They're having neuropsychological evaluations, but they're running late." The mom glanced at the admitting counter with frustration.

Vivian noticed that Skynyrd Dad had closed his eyes.

"How long have you been waiting?"

"About fifteen minutes, but they said it might be another hour." Mom dug in her diaper bag and pulled out a tissue. She reached over and wiped the nose of her Two Cute twin.

"We're waiting for my sister, Ceci," Vivian blurted,

trying to keep the lie simple and remembering a test that Jesse went through. "My niece is having an AABR," she said, chin-gesturing to Grant, who was looking at them.

Getting a quizzical look from Mom, Vivian said, "Automated Auditory Brainstem Response—they're not sure if she can hear. She's two as well."

Vivian smiled at the Two Cute twin, who looked at her. Dad folded his arms and appeared committed to a nap. Vivian said, "We've got about an hour wait time too, I guess. If your husband wants to lie down, there's a room down the hall with couches." Vivian pointed. "I could help you keep watch?"

Mom didn't hesitate; she nudged Skynyrd Dad. "Hey, there's a place down the hall with a couch. Go ahead, I'll come and get you when they're ready."

Skynyrd Dad didn't need to be asked twice. He got up and left. "He just got off work," Mom said. "It's already been a long day."

"I'm Vivian. Nice to meet you."

"I'm Sally. This one is Honoria," she said, pointing to Two Cute. "And this is her twin, Hope."

Vivian swallowed hard and gave Grant a frantic glance.

Just then, Hope woke up and began to cry. Sally went into mom mode and dug into a nearby bag and grabbed a sippy cup. Just then, Honoria bolted across the room and out of sight. Sally jumped up, looking panicked.

Vivian held out her hand for the cup and smiled. "Go ahead, I've got this."

Sally looked unsure, but she gave it to Vivian and said, "I'll be right back."

Vivian didn't hesitate but put her hand on Hope's leg with her left hand and watched her carefully as the child sipped on her juice, looking at her. Big brown eyes, both still wet from a quick tearful waking moment, looked out at her as the child paused her drinking and chewed on the spout of the cup. Hope pulled the cup away from her small mouth and smiled. Vivian smiled back.

In all, Vivian had about ten minutes alone time with Hope. Sally came back, and shortly after, their name was called. Vivian helped Sally pack up the twins and find Skynyrd.

Returning, she said to Grant, "Let's go."

In the car, she said, "How in the world am I ever going to know what happened to her? I got her last name, but it would have been weird to exchange numbers. This was a dumb idea."

"We'll just have to think of something else," Grant said, driving.

Vivian's phone beeped, indicating a text. She pulled it out of her purse and read it. "Oh wow," she said. "You know Connie? That woman I told you about from therapy? She's in a coma. They don't know what's wrong with her."

"That woman whose husband has that patent?"

"Yes," Vivian said, looking out the window as they sat in traffic not far from the hospital. "My God. I wonder what could have happened?" Vivian typed a response to their mutual friend, asking for more details.

Reading again from the phone, she said, "She's at Abbott. In ICU. My God, Grant, her children, her husband, what are they going to do?"

"They'll figure it out. She'll be okay," he said, changing lanes.

Vivian's hand flew to her mouth as her stomach flipped. "Grant! Turn around! Go back!"

"What?" he said, startled.

"Grant!" she shrieked, her face on fire. "Go to Abbott. Now! What if I did this? Oh my God, Oh my God!" She rocked back and forward.

"What are you talking about?" Grant said as he tried to maneuver the car to exit.

Vivian's eyes were saucers; her heart pounded out of her chest. "I held her! Yesterday! She hugged me! She touched me. She held my left hand."

Grant looked panicked too. "But why would she get sick? What's that got to do with you?"

Vivian was crying, her hands rubbing her face. "What if I can hurt too? When I held her I was totally pissed at her. I remember thinking terrible things about her. Just shit about what an awful woman she is!"

"Okay, okay, stay calm," he said as they exited and came to a stop. "You want to head over there and talk to her?"

"We have to!" she wailed. "What if I did this? I have to fix it!"

Grant looked out of his depth. "Okay, okay," he

said, patting the air. "We'll go."

They made the short trip to Abbott Hospital, and treading through the long corridors, eventually found their way to the ICU unit. They walked up to the nurse's station.

"I'm here to see Connie Spengali?" Vivian said. "Is she here?"

The nurse said, "Are you family?"

Vivian shot Grant a look and said, "Extended. I just need a moment with her."

The nurse considered them and said, "Why don't you go to the waiting room. I'll get her husband a message."

"Steve Spengali." Vivian nodded. "Tell him it's important and that Vivian Rees needs to see him immediately."

Grant and Vivian took a seat in the waiting room and waited. After about fifteen minutes, Steve Spengali, a small kind-looking bespectacled man walked toward them.

"Are you Vivian Rees?" he said in a hushed voice.

They stood. "I am. This is my husband, Grant. I know this is unusual, and you don't know me, but I know Connie. And Tony. From OT. We go to the same place. How is she?"

Steve nodded. "She's… they don't know. They're still running tests. They've got her on broad spectrum antibiotics, but there's some kind of infection, or something." He trailed off. "They just don't know," he barely whispered.

Vivian reached out and gently touched his arm.

"I'm so sorry, Steve. Can I see her? I... listen, I'm sorry, I know you don't know me, but Connie and I..." Vivian's eyes filled with tears. "Just for a few minutes, Steve. Please?"

"Sure," he said and turned around. They followed him to the glass doors. The three of them looked inside at young Connie Spengali, intubated, surrounded by machines. "Her parents live in California. They won't be here until tonight. Her sister lives in North Carolina. She's on standby. I've got a babysitter at the house with the kids."

"I'll wait out here," Grant said, gesturing for Vivian to go in.

"You gotta use the Purell," Steve said, indicating the dispenser outside the room.

Vivian nodded and used the antibacterial sanitizer and walked inside. She didn't waste time. Putting out her left hand, she laid it gently on Connie's arm. "Connie," she whispered. "It's me, Vivian. Vivian Rees."

Obviously not receiving a response, Vivian ran her hand down Connie's arm and held her hand with both of hers. "Connie, if I did this, please forgive me. Please forgive me. I'm so sorry. Please get better, Connie. You've got to fight this. I know you can. You're one of the strongest women I know. Your energy puts us all to shame. I'm so sorry, Connie. Please, please get better."

Vivian worked to control her emotions; she didn't want to come unglued. She moved her left hand with the ring onto Connie's head, and with everything she had, willed her to recover. She moved it again briefly, onto her chest, and then held her hand again.

Steve walked into the room. Still holding Connie's hand, she turned to look at him. "Is there anything we can do? Help with the children?"

He shook his head. "No." He stared at his wife.

Vivian looked back at Connie and gave her hand one last squeeze. "I'll see you soon," she said and released her. She walked over to Steve and bowed her head. "I'll leave my number at the nurse's station. Please call us if we can help."

They left.

Home that night, Grant and Vivian lay in bed, this time with Jesse between them. The light still on, Jesse had fallen asleep with no hat, no vest, no story, and not under a heaping mound of blankets. Just tucked between them, holding a stuffed bear. They'd watched his favorite show together as a family, and he'd simply turned over and fallen asleep.

"He's so beautiful," Vivian said, softly stroking his hair.

"He always has been," said Grant.

There was a weight to those words that stopped her. She looked at Grant. "You mean like in every way?"

He nodded. "Yes."

She thought about it and realized it was true.

Whatever affliction had or still affected him, he was perfect. There was nothing wrong with him. He was who he was meant to be.

"But he's in less pain now, Grant. You can see that, can't you?"

"Yes. I'm grateful. For him, for all of us."

Vivian lay her head on the soft pillow next to her son and stared at him. "It's a miracle. We were given a miracle."

"Yes. I think so."

They lay quietly until Grant rolled over and turned off the light. Once again, in the dark, Vivian said, "What do we do now?"

"I think we need to give it back."

Vivian blinked her eyes. Adjusted now to the dark, she could see the moon's glow through the blinds on the window. "Give it back?" she whispered.

"It may have the power to heal, but it also may have the power to destroy. We may have seen that today."

Vivian reached down and turned the ring on her finger, feeling it move freely. "But what if Jesse needs it? What if it's temporary, Grant? What if you get sick, or I get sick, or your sister, or Mom…"

"I don't think we should be greedy, Vivian. I don't think it was meant for that. If it does contain magical powers, then it knows what to do. Maybe it's waiting for the next person to find it. Maybe this is what it does? We don't own it. We shouldn't try to control it. I don't think we can."

Vivian could feel Jesse's soft breathing next to her heart. She touched him, putting her left hand on his chest. "My little love," she whispered.

And then, "Thank you, Grant."

The three of them slept.

Chapter Seven

The next day, Grant called in to work, explaining that he needed to take a few days off. They packed the car and headed for the lake. They enjoyed the travel, perhaps for the first time. It was all about Jesse. Every moment, every time they did something that would have previously elicited a violent response, they got compliance. He was just a happy kid, looking around him, experiencing life for the first time, no longer encased in a web of pain.

They unloaded the car and walked down to the lake. Grant and Jesse had on their suits, Grant chasing a giggling Jesse all the way to the beach. The three of them walked out onto the dock. A wooden bench secured onto the end platform looked out onto the clear, calm lake. The sun was still up, but early evening was upon them.

Grant and Jesse went swimming as Vivian sat and

watched. Her husband threw Jesse up in the air and caught him as they laughed and paddled about.

Vivian got a text. It was from her friend from therapy. *Connie got moved out of ICU. Recovering!*

Vivian's hand flew over her mouth as tears sprung to her eyes. Another miracle. She hadn't been too late. Grant looked over at her and swam up with Jesse, who climbed the ladder and ran down the dock toward the boathouse. Grant questioned her from the water. "What?"

"It's Connie. She's out of ICU. She's going to be okay."

Grant dropped his head and shoulders. "Thank God."

"Thank God," Vivian said. Light-headed, she removed the ring with a trembling hand and stood. She stared at the shiny, mysterious band with the indelible but allusive writing. "I guess I just put it back, huh?"

Grant climbed up onto the dock and grabbed a towel. He wrapped it around him as they looked at it together. "Just cast it away."

She looked at her strong husband and glanced back toward the boathouse. Jesse had a small bucket and was bending over, putting something special in it. His small green water wings still on, he looked happy.

She brought the ring to her lips and kissed it. "Thank you," she said. Looking out onto the bright water, the evening sun making the surface white bright, she flung it out and watched as the sun grabbed one last chance to gleam brightly off it before, with a very soft plunk, it disappeared.

Grant took hold of her hand. "It will surface again."

She squeezed back. "Yes."

Acknowledgements

Although this book is obviously a work of fiction, it was inspired by my life as a special needs mom. My son's diagnosis—or the "A word"—is spoken in hushed tones in our house, as well as the impetus and anxiety to share that part of my life with my readers. But here it is.

My other fiction is fun and meant to give readers a respite from anxiety. I've reveled in the luxury of those fantasies and find the escape into writing a significant blessing. I also write a scathing blog where I take no prisoners. That too, is cathartic. You should try it!

But it all stems from who I am and my journey as a mother. The chronic grief of having a child with special needs has left its impression on my soul. And I, like parents everywhere, share a rollercoaster of emotions as I work through my life with the hopeful prayer that I am doing my best.

If only, are words that haunt me. My beautiful son and I will forever travel together and my love, if not my magical ability to cure him, will remain true.

Thank you to the multitude of specialists, teachers, counselors, friends, and family who we've been blessed to have in our lives. Thank you to my husband. You've been a rock... for all of us. And to my other child, my lovely and adored daughter.... when I pass, may all my strength and love pass to you. We thank you.

About the Author

Annabelle Lewis is a pseudonym for the author who lives in Minneapolis with her husband, son, and a wild thug of a dog who keeps life in perspective.

She very much appreciates your reviews. You can reach Annabelle and follow her blog at:

www.theannabellelewis.com

Annabellelewisauthor@gmail.com

Twitter:
@alewisauthor

Facebook:
www.facebook/com/Annabellelewisauthor

www.ingramcontent.com/pod-product-compliance
Lightning Source LLC
Chambersburg PA
CBHW071136100726
47908CB00008B/2619